Glass

Julie Haydon

NELSON
CENGAGE Learning

Australia • Brazil • Japan • Korea • Mexico • Singapore • Spain • United Kingdom • United States

Lots of things
are made of glass.

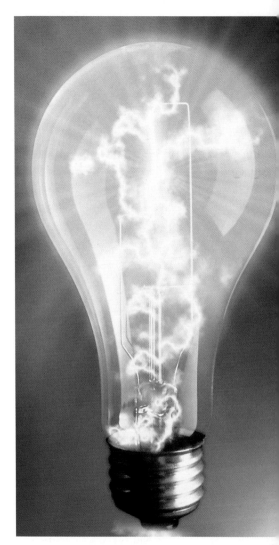

Glass is all around us.
Where does glass
come from?

We make glass.

We make glass from sand.

We make glass at a factory.

At the glass factory,
the sand goes
into a furnace.

The furnace is
like a big oven.

The furnace
is so hot that
the sand melts.

The sand becomes
hot glass.

Hot glass is soft.

It looks like honey.

11

Hot glass
can be made
into different
shapes and sizes.

It can be made

into bottles

and bowls.

When glass cools,

it becomes hard.

Glass can be many different colours.

Lots of things are
made of glass.

Glass is all around us.